Man:
It's What's for Dinner
By Mike Baeske

Illustration by Ashley Sharp

1

Ringing. Horrible, horrible ringing. You hit the alarm with your hoof and go back to blissful sleep, dreaming of Babe and her beautiful snout. You are almost to the good part of your usual fantasy, the part where the two of you enter the surf and start the heavy petting as the sun begins to set, when the ringing starts back up again. At first you try to ignore it, but the alien noise reverberating over the water really ruins the mood. You smack the alarm clock harder this time and try to head back to where you left off.

Back in your state of slumber, you look around but your girlfriend is nowhere to be seen. The entire ocean has also vanished, replaced by a misty forest. You are running through the trees with barely enough light to discern the trail that you are following. The sound of your hooves rustling through last fall's leaves is the only audible noise, which means you either lost your prey or it has collapsed.

You enter a clearing and see your dad standing over the 12 pointer you shot. Dad is smiling. No, smirking, as if he knows that you don't want to see him right now.

Way to go subconscious! You take a hot and steamy dream and then throw my dad in its place. Kudos to you!

Suddenly a group of feral humans come out of the woods. Somehow, they have laser rifles and miniguns. They nod at your dad and point their guns at you. You have no idea why humans would be working with your dad and you don't stay to find out. You run in the opposite direction. Laser blasts tear through the woods around you. You can hear the high pitched shriek of the shots barely missing your head. A dead log bursts into flames in front of you as a blue rifle blast hits it. You turn left trying to avoid the shots. There are green glowing blast marks in the trunks of the trees where minigun rounds made contact. The forest floor becomes steep. You trip and start rolling down the hill, hitting tree trunks and thorn bushes as you go.

The alarm rings again.

I might as well get ready now. Can't get back to the good dream, anyways.

You turn off the alarm, sit up, and start rubbing your hooves over your eyelids. After letting out an exceptionally long yawn, you step out of bed and walk into the restroom, being careful not to lose your balance in the process. Trying to walk on two hooves in the morning without wearing a nanosuit is a bit cumbersome, but having a fully charged suit is well worth avoiding last year's incident. Other students still bring up the time you ran out of class half naked as your nanosuit started to lose power and drip onto the floor, despite how hard you wish to forget about it.

After using the restroom and taking a shower, you stop and stare at your reflection in the mirror. Your pink skin is darker than normal due to your preference to having the hottest shower possible. The peach fuzz hair covering your entire body is getting longer than your hooves, which means it is about time for a shave. You check the corner of your blue eyes for that mysterious gunk that accumulates during the night, but it looks like the shower cleaned that up. Your right triangular ear is bent at a weird angle, probably from when you were drying yourself, so you flip it back to its normal upright state. The exterior of you snout looks fine, but you open your mouth and stare at your teeth.

Life would be so much easier if I had tusks. It sucks that I was born a Pigian. I would have made a great Boaron. Even if I had the smallest tusks ever recorded, it still would have been better than being a no-tusked Pigian.

You turn to your side, making your

robust potbelly more noticeable.

Things could be worst, though. The ladies do love my potbelly. I am not a total waste of space.

You walk over to the nanosuit prep station and step onto the hoof marks, which simultaneously depresses the markings and causes the nanomites to come out of the station. You know the nanomites are tiny robots, but to your eyes it looks like living liquid mercury is sliding up your body. As the nanomites crawl up your skin, it feels like your skin is being dipped in freezing cold water as the nanomites connect to your nervous system. Normally you turn off the majority of the sensory functionality in your suit because you don't like the feeling of being nude in public, especially after the incident.

Your entire body below your neck looks like it is coated in liquid metal now. The chill keeps moving up the back of your spine as the nanomites attempt to connect directly with your brain. Loud metallic clanging starts rattling throughout the room as the robots connect with your auditory receptors then the normal ambient noise returns. The room flickers in and out of sight with oscillating total darkness and blinding light until finally the whole room vanishes and you are looking at the Nanoswine logo: a half robot, a half Boaron with a rifle in one hoof and the caption "Get Nanoswine or get shot. It is your choice." just below him.

Once the logo fades away, the suit starts changing colors and textures. One second it looks like polished onyx, the next it takes the shape of fur with a kaleidoscope of colors. Every few seconds the suit and your body completely vanish as it tests the cloaking mode. The testing goes on for minutes. Sometimes the combinations it makes are appealing and you wish you can remember them, other times you wish you can forget the atrocities it forms. You try not to stare directly at the shifting for too long; because, if you do, you will continue to see those changing shapes even when you close your eyes. The suit finishes the testing and returns to its neutral state of looking like liquid mercury.

For many people, choosing the right look in the morning is a major task due to the infinite options available with nanosuits, but that has never been a problem for you. You have a set of favorites that you normally wear, all of which were designed by other people. Most of your favorites look like armor that could be worn into battle, including your absolute favorite outfit which is black and has massive spikes.

The outfit you choose today is one of the few that doesn't completely look like armor. The upper half of the suit looks like a green and silver striped t-shirt from afar, but on closer inspection the silver stripes are literally made of a polished metal while the green stripes are made of alligator hide. The lower half of the nanosuit also has patches of alligator hide, but it is surrounded by metallic weaves that look like a bunch of partially exposed electrical wires entwined.

God, I am starving. I better get some food. The only thing worse than going to class is going to class hungry.

2

As you walk toward the kitchen to get breakfast, your eyes wander into the living room toward the trophies over the fireplace. Three human heads are mounted on plaques just above the mantel. Two of the trophies belong to your dad, but the newest one belongs to you and is located in the prominent central position.

As mounted heads go, yours is nearly perfect. The hairline is bald, but still has grey hair on the sides to prove the human's authenticate age. The eyebrows are so thick, bushy, and grey that they look like two tiny anorexic chinchillas. Matching the eyebrows, the nostril hairs are thick and long. A few of the teeth in the mouth are missing, but the remaining ones are all a shade of mustard yellow with signs of decay scattered throughout.

I still can't believe I shot a 12 point brute. What are the odds of me finding and killing such a majestic beast, especially on my first hunting trip? It is going to be hard to top that one.

You walk into the kitchen where Mom is making lunch. She is cutting a meat loaf with a laser as it float in the air. The first time you saw her nanosuit levitate an object, you thought it was magic, but nowadays the maglev technology is just a normal occurrence.

"Good morning Wilbur. Did you sleep well?"

"Good morning Mom. Yeah, not bad."

You start making some toast and get a container of ovarian jelly out of the refrigerator. The container states in big bold letters, "A great source of iron!"

"It sounded like you were up pretty late. I hope you can still pay attention in class today."

And so it begins …

"I should be fine. I wasn't up that late."

"It was at least 1 am. What were you doing that couldn't wait for today?"

Talking to Babe.

"Anatomy homework."

The toast is finished cooking. You apply a coat of the crimson ovarian jelly onto the bread.

"Do you normally talk that much when doing homework?" She stares at you with her piercing eyes.

"I learn the names of the body parts better when I say them out loud."

Not completely a lie. I was talking about body

parts last night, but she would kill me if she knew which ones they were.

"Right ... I am sure we will see that hard work pay off when we get your final Anatomy grade."

"Mom, that tone hurts. It is as if you don't believe your favorite child and I must say that it is troubling. You really should work on your trust issues."

Mom's eyes are on fire now. The last sentence may have hit too close to home.

"What I believe is that you should work on your homework, instead of talking to your girlfriend all night long."

You force yourself to take a bite of your toast. The ovarian jelly gives it a nice meaty flavor, but it is impossible to enjoy the taste with how this conversation is going.

I am still breathing, so she didn't hear what I was saying last night. These are just blind accusations. Deny. Deny. Deny.

"I am glad to hear your true feelings come out now, but your assumption is wrong. I wish I had been speaking to Babe last night because I am sure it would have been more fun than homework."

Indeed it was.

Mom shakes her head and turns around to continue making her lunch. You finish eating the rest of the toast.

Disaster averted.

A rattling noise is coming from behind the counter. Spike must have woken up from that conversation. You stretch over the counter and see him shaking the metal bars of his cage, which is his customary sign of wanting out. Mom keeps preparing her lunch, either not noticing Spike or not caring. You let out a loud sigh, walk over to the cage, and release him. He crawls out of the cramped cage and slowly stands up.

Spike is a 27 year old human that your family got five years ago from a human breeder. You had begged your parents for years to get a pet human, but they had always been against it. Mom had always said she was allergic to human dander, while Dad did not want to put up with the hassle and cost of owning a pet, but eventually they caved in and bought one; although it was neither the breed nor age you wanted. They got a discount for how old he was; most customers want potty trained toddlers, which are much cuter.

Spike puts his hands around his throat.

"I know that you are thirsty. Hold on a minute. I am getting it for you," you say while fetching a bowl of water for him. Spike's stomach growls as you walk back to him.

Oops, did I feed him last night? I was wondering why he kept bugging me while I talked to Babe. I guess he didn't want to play after all. Kicking that tennis ball at him may have been a bit unwarranted...

You put the bowl on the ground. He picks it up and starts gulping down the water, while you command the nanomites to form a pair of pincers at the end of your hoof. You open up a cabinet and pull out a can of Yum Yums. As you open the can, you notice the label says it is made with 40% real chicken.

Gross. I can't believe they eat birds.

You plop the contents of the can in a bowl and set it on the ground next to Spike. He starts shoveling it into his mouth and within seconds it is all gone, except for the disgusting yellow grime around his lips.

Wow, that was impressive.

"Why did Spike devour his food like that? Did you forget to feed him last night?"

Of course, now you pay attention to him at the most inconvenient time.

"I don't know. Why don't you ask him? Oh wait, you can't because you had his voice box clipped."

"Nice try. Do you really want a pet that talks back to you and complains about how you didn't feed him last night?"

Not really. It would be creepy.

"We could have given him a chance, instead of having it clipped before we even took him home."

"That would have only hurt your cause right now. Do you want me to ask him if he was fed last night? I bet he will shake his head no."

"Ok, I may have forgotten to give him food, but it is stupid that we don't allow him to get his own food and water, anyways."

"Wilbur, I can't believe you. Do you have any idea how rare a purebred Cherokee is? Not to mention how expensive he was to get. I hate to think of what would happen if Dad and I went on vacation. We would come back and Spike would be dead in his cage."

"Mom, you were the one who wanted a Cherokee, so don't guilt trip me about how expensive Spike was! I said I wanted an Indian, as in a human from India. They have a completely different look and attitude."

"Wilbur, it doesn't matter what breed he is; you still should have fed him last night!"

"I can't change the past, Mom; despite what you heard. I fed him this morning and that is the best I can do. It isn't like I intentionally tried to starve him. Anyways, I have to go or I will be late for class."

"Hold up, I made you lunch."

First time for everything.

"Thanks," you say as you look inside the bag. "Dragon fingers?"

"Yes, there are some dipping sauces in there too."

"I appreciate it, but do we always have to eat Chinese? Can't we mix it up sometimes?"

"Once you get a job, you can buy all the

expensive food you want. Chinese is what we can afford on a regular basis."

"Are we still on for Dad's birthday dinner tonight?" you ask as you start to walk out the door.

"Yes. Make sure you are at the restaurant by six and you can have whatever you want. As long as it is Chinese," Mom jokes.

"Very funny Mom," you say as the door closes shut.

You walk toward your hovercraft, a model 42 H2G2, which looks like the shell of a horseshoe crab. Back in the day it was a decent midlevel hovercraft with a silver paintjob and a state of the art autopilot system, but that was fifty years before you were born. Now it is more rust than machine. As you approach the door, your nanosuit starts up the hovercraft and opens up the driver side door.

"Make sure you use your autopilot!" Mom shouts from the front door of the house.

"Whatever you say, Mom."

What is the point of finally being allowed to drive when you just let the computer do it for you? Where is the fun in that?

You sit down on the leather seat, which now has some large holes in the human skin from years of use, and the door closes behind you. Your nanosuit starts showing the different gauges of the hovercraft, including the remaining fuel, current speed, altitude of the craft, cabin temperature and a map of the streets around you. You instruct it to only show the speed, the altitude, and the map. A warning message takes up your sight saying that autopilot should be used at all times to prevent injury or death. You acknowledge the message and force it into manual control.

It is almost as bad as my mom.

3

You start driving to Squealer's place. In the distance, you can see the Chicago Barrier, but from this far away it looks like a snow globe. To the right, a neighbor is walking her 3 year old human on a choker leash. Her pet is pooping in the grass and there is no sign that she is going to clean it up.

So Miss Hamm is the culprit who lets her human shit in our yard. Good to know. I have a new place to take Spike when he needs to do his business. See if she likes that new lawn ornament in-between her plaster gnomes.

It is a five minute drive to get to Squealer's house. You activate the radio to pass the time. A broadcaster says, "Breaking news: three slain Hogonians were found today at the east side of New Swine City. Neighbors reported screaming and feral human sightings earlier in the day. Human Control was spotted on the scene, but refused to comment on the ongoing investigation."

You turn off the radio.

Nevermind.

A sign to your right catches your eye. It says, "Come visit Sammy the Samoan at the New Swine City Zoo." Below the caption is a picture of a large human who is covered in tattoos. He is standing in a cage that has artificial palm trees, a stream made with sand and rocks, and some beer cans scattered on the ground to add a better sense of realism.

That is impressive. I wonder how they knew what his natural environment looked like.

As you get closer to your destination, the houses get more luxurious, making your home look like a shack. Your family has never had much money, considering your dad is an exterminator and your mom is a nurse at the local hospital, but you wouldn't say you are poor. Squealer's parents have more money than they can handle. His dad is a heart surgeon and his mom enjoys spending his earnings. Thankfully the two of you met when you were piglets, when money was as meaningless as girls, so your friendship was allowed to blossom before such trivial things could squash your relationship.

You pull through the gate of Squealer's driveway and park next to his father's fountain, a female Hogonian with water coming out of every nipple (a real classy piece of art). You send Squealer a message saying that you are at his place. After a little bit, you realize that you are still staring at the fountain.

Stop being a perv, Wilbur.

You avert your eyes toward the front door, where Squealer emerges. Compared to other Pigians he is a bit scrawny, borderline sickly. He doesn't have a problem eating; but, for whatever reason, he was cursed with a high metabolism that doesn't allow him to put on the pounds. On a daily basis Squealer is ridiculed by others, normally Boarons, about his weight. You try not to bring it up.

Squealer runs toward the hovercraft. From the look on his face, something is bothering him. It is very rare for him to get upset. Normally the world walks all over him and all he says is thank you; but when he does get upset, it is very transparent. You open up the door for him and he jumps inside.

"Girls are crazy," he says.

"Good morning to you, too."

You start driving toward the university.

"Morning. Last night, Misery would not stop bugging me about when I will move out of my parents place. I haven't even graduated yet. How am I supposed to afford a place of my own?"

"You can't."

"Exactly, but does she care? No. It is all 'Life would be so much better if we lived together' and 'We could be doing this right now, if we had our own place' or 'Are you going to live with your folks for the rest of your life?' It is driving me crazy."

"Yeah, I hear that. Babe is always bringing up vegetarianism with me. It gets old quick. Thankfully she had something else on her mind last night, though."

"I did notice those fights happening more often between you two lately. Are you worried that she is going to make you choose between her and meat?"

"I know she loves me, but yeah I think it might come down to that. It was never an issue before, but nowadays it seems to always be on her mind, especially when we eat meals together."

"That is rough. I don't think I could give up meat; it is too delicious. If she gave you an ultimatum right now, which way would you go?"

"I am not sure. I think I could give up meat if I wanted to, but there would be a bigger issue at hoof. I don't make demands like that to Babe, so why should she? That could be a deal breaker, if she did go that route. What are you going to do with the living situation and Misery?"

"Drink more. That way I can endure the endless nagging and ridicule," Squealer says with a smile.

"That is one option."

"If that doesn't work, I am not sure what I will do. Sometimes I feel like I could do better than her. That I deserve someone better than her."

"Yeah, that is an understatement."

"What do you mean by that?" Squealer asks.

"You definitely deserve better than her. She is constantly using you for her own personal gain, belittling you to feel better about herself, and controlling you to compensate for her own unmanageable life. If I were you, I would have called it quits on the first date, before the appetizer arrived. You are a saint for lasting as long as you have."

Plus she is exactly like your mom and that is just weird.

"Please don't hold anything back. I would hate to see you hurt yourself by holding onto some of those negative feelings you have toward my girlfriend."

"You're lucky I didn't talk about her looks. I held that back, just in case you do continue to date her for awhile."

"She definitely is no Babe…"

"Yeah…"

If only she was okay with me eating meat.

You pass by a Piglet's Manshack sign. Initially it shows a smiling piglet, but then it fades to black and a video starts playing. A peppy girl announcer says, "Come to Piglet's

Manshack today and enjoy our Mexican fest. For a limited time only, try our dynamite quesadillas or sizzling fajitas for only 57 credits. All made with our 100 % grade A Mexican meat, which is organically raised in Ottawa." The video ends with two humans frolicking over green pastures, while holding hands.

Seriously, who gives a shit about whether they were raised nicely or not? I don't want to hear that my dinner lived a happy life. If anything, I want to hear that it lived the worst life imaginable and that I am doing it a favor by eating it.

"So what are you and Babe doing for lunch today? Misery and I are thinking about picking up food from Chinese Express," Squealer says.

"I brought some finger food, so we will probably eat near the pond. I am not a fan of Chinese Express, anyways. I heard sometimes when you order the General Tso that it isn't actually man, but chicken. That is just gross."

"No way, they have regulations against that. Are you sure it wasn't cat or dog? Avian meat would get that place closed in a heartbeat."

"I am just saying that is what I heard. Better to be safe than eating something that clucks."

"Thanks a lot. Chinese Express is one of my favorites and now I am always going to be paranoid about eating their food."

"That is nothing compared to what is in

marshmallows."

"Shut up."

"Seriously, I have seen how much you like Tots. You will never be able to look at those baby shaped marshmallows again, if you knew what was in them."

"Wilbur, I am warning you: do not say one more bad thing about Tots. I don't care what is in them. You know how much I love them."

"I know, but I feel it is my moral obligation as your friend to tell you that marshmallows contain … ow! You didn't have to hit me."

"I warned you. It is my moral obligation to beat you up if you speak ill of Tots again."

"Your morals are completely out of whack."

"You're one to talk."

"Dog bones."

"What did you call me?" Squealer asks.

"They boil the skeletons of dogs and the remaining liquid solidifies into the gelatin in marshmallows. Babe made me watch a video on it and I am now scarred for life."

"What type of monster comes up with that idea and puts it into candy?"

"Humans use to do the same thing, only using pigs and cattle. I think we got the idea from them."

"No surprise there. They also use to club

baby seals and wear their fur as coats, but that doesn't mean it is a good idea."

"True," you say as something runs in front of the hovercraft. Before you can avoid the creature, it hits the front of the hovercraft and gets sucked underneath. The crunching sound of the creature being squashed by the hovercraft's jets sends a chill down your spine.

"Holy shit," you scream as you slam on the brakes and pull to the side of the road.

"What was that?" asks Squealer.

"This is not happening. Please tell me this is not happening. Was that a person?"

You look behind you at the mass lying on the road. Half of it is flattened like a pancake and there is a pool of blood growing around the body. Your stomach starts to turn sour and it is getting hard to breath.

Oh my God, my life is over. I should have used the autopilot.

The skin is pink, so it must be a Pigian. An arm is visible, which means the lower half of the body was squashed. From your angle, you can't make out what the head looks like. The arm is rather long for a Pigian and the hoof doesn't look normal. It isn't a hoof.

"Thank God, it is just a human," you exhale.

"What?"

"It doesn't have hooves; it has hands, so it must be a human. I thought my life was over.

That I was going to be convicted for involuntary slaughter and would be sent to an asteroid prison for the rest of my life. Thankfully it was just a stupid human. Let's get out of here," you say as you start driving again.

"Is it still alive?" Squealer asks.

"Doubt it. Did you see the lower half of its body?"

"Yeah, it was horrible."

"Agreed. That is a perfect example of why population control is necessary. Babe doesn't believe in hunting to thin the numbers, but look what happens with our current number of feral humans, let alone letting the population grow without thinning the herd."

"Whatever you say," Squealer replies.

"Don't get me wrong; I hate that I killed it, but it shouldn't have ran out on the street like that. There was nothing I could have done."

"I wonder what would have happened if you had been using the autopilot. Would it still be alive?"

"Probably the same thing, but if it would make you feel better, I will turn on the autopilot for the rest of the drive," you say. You command the nanosuit to start the autopilot on the hovercraft. An awkward silence fills the vehicle. For the rest of the drive, no one talks. You keep thinking about the accident, how it could have been prevented, and what would have happened if it was a person you had hit.

Your vehicle pulls into Hogington University. There are fifteen buildings at your school, five parking sites for hovercrafts, and two landing bays for flying vehicles. There are never enough parking spaces for the number of students enrolled, which wouldn't be that big of a deal if you arrived early, but that never works out. All the parking areas must be taken near your class, because the autopilot heads toward the north parking lot. The roads are filled with hovercrafts and speeder bikes, while shuttles, cruisers, and gliders fill the sky, as students try to beat the clock.

You pass the main building on campus, the Scholar's Tower. It is the largest building in town, over eighty stories high, and is made from a crimson metal found in the asteroid belt circling Hogart, the Hogonian's home planet. The tower is where all the teachers' offices are and where most of the graduate classes are held. You have never been inside it and probably never will, but its outside is impressive, nonetheless.

"Sorry about the accident this morning. Thankfully neither one of us was hurt, but it could have gone differently," you say to Squealer.

"Don't worry about it. It wasn't your fault and like you said it was just a stupid human. See you in anatomy class," says Squealer.

"See yah."

There is ten minutes before your class starts, which is completely across campus. You have already been late three times this semester, which is not that shocking considering it is an 8 am class, and you will lose a letter grade if you are tardy again. You don't have the luxury to lose that grade, you are barely passing.

Time to high tail it out of here.

Getting to class wouldn't be too hard, except there are five roads in-between this parking lot and your destination. Five roads filled with students who are driving like a pig on fire because they are also running late. Every time you do try to cross, you have flashbacks to one of your favorite video games. In the game you are human needing to cross a major highway to get to the chicken on the other side. If you get run over, you lose, but that was always your favorite part because of the cool animations that would occur depending on how you were hit and by what type of vehicle. Now it isn't so cool considering that you are the human in this scenario.

You have no choice but to walk first and pray that the drivers are paying attention. While you cross the first road, a Warty on a speeder bike has to stop suddenly. She is short and hairy like all Warties. She tells you to go screw yourself. She also mentions something about your mother, a brute, and a duck, but it doesn't make much sense.

The rest of the roads don't give you too much trouble. You walk in front of a couple of drivers but none of them yell at you nor mention a duck and your Mom in the same sentence. As you pass by different students, you check out their online profiles. Most of the girl profiles are blocked, while almost all the guys allow you to see everything.

4

You get to class, with a minute to spare, and find the closest seat to the door that is still available.

The teacher, Miss Piggy, stands up at exactly 8 am. She is the oldest Hogonian that you have ever seen. All of her hair is grey and every centimeter of her skin is wrinkled. When she takes a break from talking, you sometimes wonder if she finally passed away.

"I will start with an easy question today, considering that most of you look groggy. Which species discovered Earth?" Miss Piggy asks.

A Hogonian in the front row raises her hoof. She always has the answers to the review questions. You envision her reading the material as soon as she gets home and only stopping before heading to class an hour early. No one really likes her, including the teacher. Miss Piggy hesitates to see if someone else will raise their hoof and then selects the Hogonian know-it-all.

"Hogonians discovered Earth after noting an abnormal solar flare from the local star. Our scientists monitored this solar system from a distance for many years without realizing life was present; until a group of scientists flew through this solar system for a research experiment and happened to scan this planet," the girl smugly says.

"Correct and you just so happened to answer my next question. Now, can anyone else tell me, how was Earth monitored after the discovery of life?" Miss Piggy asks.

The Hogonian girl raises her hoof again, despite Miss Piggy's clear wording. A Boaron to the left of you also raises his hoof. Miss Piggy selects him and the know-it-all begrudgingly lowers her hoof.

"Initially, we monitored the human's radio transmissions from a distance. Eventually, we also monitored them from cloaked ships in Earth's thermosphere," the Boaron says.

"Very good. Who can tell me the circumstances of the first human meal?"

A Warty in the back row raises his hoof. The teacher looks shocked to see him volunteer to answer. She selects him.

"It happened during the Vietnam War. An elite covert group of Warties were testing the humans' tactics, when one of the operatives got hungry. The Warty cooked the human on his own fire pit and shared the meat with the rest of the squad," the Warty answers.

"There were Boarons in that group as well, but besides that you are correct. That was the last topic we discussed before class let out on Tuesday. Today we will be covering the invasion of Earth," Miss Piggy says.

Okay, I am going to pay attention and do well in this class.

Miss Piggy starts up her presentation. She tends to go with plain text slides with the bare minimum amount of pictures and videos. The slides are perfect for cramming for tests, but they are also as exciting as watching slugs race.

"I won't name names; but some professors who teach this class tend to spend an excessive amount of time covering the battles of the invasion of Earth and the rest of the semester is skimped over. I will not do you that disservice. For those of you more interested in such barbaric things, there is a History of Warfare class taught every two years."

God, I wish I was in that class right now. Why are all the good classes only taught every two years? It is like the school systems intentionally make it impossible to take the interesting classes, while the most boring ones are readily available every semester.

"The first phase of the invasion was code named operation Clean Sweep. At 2:00 am CST, cloaked ships emitted high-altitude electromagnetic pulses across the entire planet. The atmospheric EMP strike was more powerful than anything previously seen on Earth; it disabled every satellite and destroyed all advanced technology. Over 90% of the human's weaponry was rendered useless through the initial strike," Miss Piggy says in a slow, monotone voice. Your eyelids are getting heavy.

Okay, new goal: I am going to stay awake in class today.

"The second phase of the invasion focused on containment. Our Boaron leaders wanted to trap the humans in the major cities that they already infested. Within minutes of the EMP attacks, energy shields, like the Chicago Barrier, were established in every metropolis on the planet, trapping over 60% of humans into easily farmable populations. The human trafficking industry was officially born as soon as the barrier went up," the teacher drones on as the other students start to drift into sleep or daydreams.

This is unbearable. There should be a law against teachers who speak in a monotone voice. This stuff might actually be interesting, if the delivery was better.

"After capturing the cities, the Boarons confronted the remaining militaries of the planets. Laser canons from the space fleet were utilized to destroy military facilities, while aircrafts targeted any vehicles outside of the blast radius. The majority of the humans' combat vehicles were disabled through the EMP attack, but that damage could be repaired, so all combat vehicles were 'neutralized', as the Boarons would say. By the end of the first day of the invasion, all military bases were destroyed and Earth was effectively under Boaron control," Miss Piggy says.

I wonder what Babe is doing right now. I really should know her schedule, but I keep forgetting it.

"That is not to say that the fighting was over, far from it. As you all well know, feral humans are still a problem today, but back then they were the strongest that they would ever be. Back then, they had massive stockpiles of ammo to resist their new rulers and the naïveté to think that they could still win."

Yesterday, she worked, so today she either has off or has class. Most likely she is off right now and sleeping. I wish I was too.

"On the opposite side of things, a continuous stream of humans surrendered to their new rulers after the first day of the invasion. Makeshift barriers were setup as concentration camps for the peaceful humans. Eventually the children and healthy mature adults were shipped off planet to start man farms on planets closer to our home planets. Healthy humans that were beyond the optimum age of breeding became slave labor and helped build the first cities inhabited by swinekind on Earth. Those that couldn't be used as slaves were either made into food or euthanized," the teacher says.

Your eyes are barely open now.

"The first civilians landed on Earth, four days after the initial invasion. The group consisted of five Hogonian scientists and twenty Pigian servants. The scientists were brought to the planet to ensure the barriers were operating as designed. The servants came to ensure the warlords were happy in..."

You fall asleep.

You are in a glider, dropping plasma bombs down upon the humans on the ground. The explosions shine bright purple and cause a high pitched shriek every time they burst. Anything caught in the blast radius is instantly disintegrated. A tank was cut in half by one of your bombs where the edges of the metal is still shining the same bright purple as the explosions. The ant sized humans flee from your aircraft as they see your path of destruction. You look to your right and see that Babe is your copilot, but you don't stop the bombing; you can't stop. She doesn't say a word, but the look in her eyes is of pure hatred.

The look of hatred wakes you up. There is a pool of drool on the desk. You slowly sit back up and discretely wipe the remaining drool off your face. Miss Piggy is still talking, so you didn't sleep too long. You wipe the puddle off your desk and notice your reflection. You have a red mark across the right side of your face from where you slept.

I hope I wasn't snoring again.

"The main human resistance leader from this region was a blond haired brute named Duke. At the peak of his rule, he had over five thousand humans under his command. For two years, Duke was the most wanted human on the planet."

Looking around, the only student still paying attention is the Hogonian in the front of the class. She is completely engorged in this Duke character or just the environment of being taught some meaningless historical information that has no relevance in daily life. Nonetheless, you make a mental note to review the missed material before the test, even though, the likelihood of that happening is as good as you spontaneously growing tusks.

"Next time, we will cover the defeat of Duke at the battle of Hamilton. Please do not forget about your essay assignment which is due next Thursday. Late submissions will not be accepted," the teacher says as students begin to walk out the door.

There goes my weekend. That does sound familiar now that she mentioned it. Maybe Babe will help me write it. She is always better at that crap. Probably because she is a psychology major which automatically gives her the supernatural power of understanding what the teacher actually wants.

5

You head toward your next class.
Squealer is waiting for you outside the building.

"How was class?" he asks.

"Boring as ever. How was yours?"

The two of you start walking.

"Another riveting accounting lecture. By the way, you have a red mark on your face."

"Yeah, I fell asleep again. Miss Piggy can cure the worst case of insomnia."

"I heard that about her. Thankfully I have never had a class with her. Any good dreams?"

"No, not really."

You receive a message from Babe through your nanosuit, "Good morning. I hope your day goes well. Do you have time for lunch?"

You reply, "Good morning. I do. I brought my own lunch today, so want to meet at the pond after my lab? "

". . . and then I am going to finally catch

up on my sleep. What are your plans tonight?" Squealer asks.

"After my internship, I am going to have dinner with my parents then homework and sleep."

You enter the lab. There are twenty black tables in the room with metal stools surrounding them. On top of each table are dissection kits, including laser braces for making incisions, and a sink. The student teacher is sitting down next to a large table that is covered with a tarp.

Your anatomy teacher is a nice guy, but this student teacher is the worst. From the very first lab session, smugness fumed from him. He has completely forgotten that he was a student taking this class last semester. Heaven help you if you actually need to ask him a question, because his condescending response will be brutal.

As you sit at the table closest to the door, you notice Squealer's attitude has completely changed. He only took this class because it is mandatory class for you and he needed to fill his science credits. It turns out he has a very weak stomach when it comes to dissecting things.

All the other tables get filled before anyone starts sitting at yours. They all know about Squealer's condition. Eventually two Warties sit at the end of the table before class begins. They give Squealer the snake eye.

You receive a response from Babe,

"Sounds good. See you soon."

The student teacher stands up and removes the tarp. The table is covered with human heads.

This is not going to turn out good.

"Today you will be dissecting a human head; particularly you will focus on the structure of the brain and eye. You will have the standard two hours to complete the assignment and this will be on the practical exam. Grab your heads and begin." The student teacher sits back on his stool.

The other students rush to get their heads. The table is completely surrounded, so you wait a minute for the crowd to disperse. You slide the dissecting brace around your hoof. The brace looks like a metal bracelet with a triangle band connecting through the diameter. The band fits snuggly into the grooves of your hoof. At the very tip of the brace is cylindrical device that actually generates the laser beam. It integrates with your nanosuit where you can control the shape and strength of the laser by just thinking about it.

"Any preferences on the head?" you ask Squealer.

"Just make sure it is a male. Are you okay with doing the dissecting by yourself?"

"Yeah, no problem."

Why even ask? I have dissected every time this semester. I much rather do it than get vomited on again.

You walk over to the table with a dozen human heads on it. Most of the heads with the interesting birth defects and scarring have already been picked over, but there are a few decent ones left.

That one with the giant nose isn't too bad, but the rest of the head is pretty boring.

At the table to the right, a Hogonian girl is making her human's mouth move. "Feed me. I am so hungry. I haven't eaten since I was decapitated and that was weeks ago," she says for the head. Everyone at her table is erupting into laughter.

"Gandhi, I am sorry but we don't have any food. The best we can do is put you out of your misery by removing your brain and chopping it into little pieces," says a Boaron at the table.

"Cut it out. You are wasting time and will not get an extension on this assignment," scolds the student teacher.

"I hate that guy. He is such a pompous jerk. I bet he has a hot date with his right hoof after class," whispers the Boaron to his group, resulting in muffled laughter. The student teacher scowls at their table.

You focus your attention back on the table of heads. After some additional deliberation, you decide to pick a blond haired, blue eyed male with a cleft chin. As you carry the head back to your table, you notice a Warty repeatedly stabbing his decapitated head.

Geeze, talk about having issues. That guy needs some therapy.

"Good enough?" you ask Squealer, while holding out the head.

"That will do. Let's get this over with," says Squealer. Somehow even his black spots look paler than normal.

"Remember, if you have to vomit, look away or at least aim at the student teacher."

"I will do my best," Squealer says with a faint smile.

As you start the dissection, the smell of the laser cutting through the flesh and skull is reminiscent of when the squirrel fell into the power generator at your place. That smell wasn't pleasant back when it emanated throughout the house for weeks after the vaporization, let alone now. Your stomach starts to turn sour.

Boar up. You are not vomiting today. Squealer is the one who vomits, not you, and he looks relatively okay. Well, better than he did when we dissected the heart.

After making an initial laser incision through the circumference of the skull, you remove the skull cap and place it on the counter. What you see inside is rather smooth and slimy. It doesn't look at all like the guided images.

"Am I missing something? Isn't the brain

suppose to have ridges and divided hemispheres?" you ask Squealer.

Counter to the planned vomit avoidance measures, Squealer examines the inside of the skull. As he takes a closer look, most of the other tables already have the brain out and have started labeling the different sections. All the other brains look like they are made of melded worms, unlike your brain.

Of course, I accidently pick the freak of nature that will guarantee we fail this assignment.

"I think we are looking at the Dura Mater, a leathery membrane that covers the brain. Try cutting it," Squealer weakly says as he looks at the floor.

You cut the membrane and see the underlying brain.

"Good call. This would be so much easier if I could use my nanosuit's analyzer in class," you say while removing the rest of the membrane.

"Yeah, but that is why we can't use them. Everyone would pass their classes, if we could use that feature."

"Ok, time to remove the brain. Keep your eyes down and I will try to do it as fast as possible."

With your left hoof, you lift up the frontal lobe of the brain, which feels like firm tofu. With your right hoof, you start cutting the nerves that are anchoring the brain into the skull, which sounds like carrots being cut for a salad. As you cut the nerves beneath the brain, you accidently get a whiff of the inside of the skull, which smells like Mom's meat and cabbage stew.

I better hurry up with this dissection and get to lunch; otherwise, I might be tempted to take a bite out of this nasty head. I doubt that will help me pass this class.

You finish cutting the nerves, lift the brain out of the skull cavity, and place it on the counter. It makes a plopping noise similar to Spike's canned chicken. After noting some of the key structures of the brain, you cut along the Corpus callosum and divide the brain into the two hemispheres.

Weird. The inside of it looks like a freaky maze that a parasitic worm would navigate through.

Finding most of the key structures is easy but you have the hardest time finding the pineal gland, a small endocrine gland that is supposed to be under the Corpus callosum and look like a tiny pine cone. After struggling for ten minutes, you realize the incision you made had torn through the pineal gland and it is dangling in a weird way.

"Now that we found that pain in the ass pineal gland, I think we have located all the key structures of the brain. On to the eyes," you say.

Squealer looks green, which is hard for someone who is pink and black.

"How are you holding up?" you ask Squealer.

"Ready for this to be over."

"We are getting there. Just hang in there a little longer."

There is no way he is going to make it through this without vomiting.

After carefully examining the guide, you instruct your nanosuit to make a tool that is like an ice cream scoop with serrated edges. You dig it into the head's right eye socket, which makes a gruesome squishing noise. The optic nerve is surprisingly stubborn and requires you to saw through it with the serrated edges of the scoop. As you severe the nerve, it gives way unexpectedly, resulting in you accidently hurling the eyeball out of its socket and against the table. The eye rolls across the table leaving a trail of blood in its wake. The eyeball almost falls off the table, but thankfully it is sticky enough that it stops just short of the edge.

A rolling eye is too much. Squealer vomits. Thankfully he does it in the sink and you can't see the vomit spewing out of his mouth, but you can hear him retching and the chunks splashing against the metal, which quickly pushes your stomach to the limit. Then the sour smell violates your nostrils. You can feel the levees break in your stomach and the flood of vomit begin to works its way out.

No, I will not be the guy who both ran out of

school naked and puked during anatomy class. One epic embarrassing moment is enough to last a lifetime.

You can taste the bile in your mouth and feel it moving up your throat, but through sheer willpower you swallow it back down. Your whole body is shaking uncontrollably, but that is an acceptable symptom. After suppressing your unruly stomach, you notice everyone is now staring at Squealer and his heaving is the only noise in the room.

Poor guy. It is bad enough having to blow chunks, let alone having a whole classroom gawking at you while it happens.

Although Squealer only vomits for a minute, it feels like forever. He eventually runs out of ammo and is left with dry heaving. The rest of your classmates return to their dissecting, while discussing the pre-lunch show they just witnessed, of course. You pick up the stray eye and move it closer to the decapitated head. Squealer turns on the sink to wash his stomach contents away.

"Are you feeling any better?" you ask Squealer.

"Yeah, sorry about that."

"Don't worry about it. I was close to doing the same thing. I hate this assignment, but we still have a bit to go. Are you up to finishing or do you need to head out?"

"Let's finish. I am not a quitter."

"My boar! Let's teach this eye who is the boss."

You start by slicing the cornea and draining the aqueous humor, a liquid that supplies nutrients between the cornea and the lens, into a vial. You then remove the still attached muscle around the eye, pierce the outside of the eye, the sclera, and cut around the circumference. After cutting away the front half of the eye from the back, you scoop the jelly like vitreous humor into its own labeled dish. The remaining eye looks like a tiny deflated beach ball. You then take the front half of the eye and surgically remove the iris and lens, putting them into their own labeled dishes.

Once the labeling is complete, the two of you clean up your lab area as fast as physically possible. You dispose of all the chunks and wipe off most of the liquids, but you would definitely never eat off of that table. You exit the lab ten minutes late.

Misery is waiting for Squealer. The very sight of her makes you want to drop kick a piglet. Her name and outward appearance are perfectly suited toward her vile personality. While girth is desired throughout swinekind, there is still such a thing as too fat and Misery goes way beyond that line. If a scientist was to dissect her, they would find that her arteries are filled with nacho cheese and onion rings.

"Took you long enough," she says.

"Sorry, Honey, we had to dissect a human's head today and it took awhile," Squealer apologizes.

"Did you vomit again?" asks Misery loudly.

A group of students start laughing and whispering to themselves as Squealer blushes.

"Yes," he says quietly.

"Oh my God, not again. Keep your distance from me. I don't want to smell it on your breath and don't even think about kissing me."

Well, at least he lucked out there. He should vomit more often to avoid kissing that beast.

"How's it going Misery?" you ask her, trying to get the embarrassing topic away from Squealer.

"Oh, hi, Wilbur. I didn't recognize you with your nanosuit on. Did I miss your daily nude run out of class?"

The same group of students burst into laughter. It sounds like they mentioned your name in their latest whispering.

"Nope, not today. I didn't want to overwhelm the girls with my amazingly good looks. Did you end up getting your sex change operation yet?"

She glares at you but doesn't have a retort.

"I am hungry. Let's get out of here, Squealer," she says.

"Oh, are you going to treat him to lunch today?"

"Real funny, Wilbur," she says while still glaring at you.

Actually it is rather sad. He really does deserve someone better than you.

Squealer gives you a shrug. "See you later," he says as he gets dragged away.

"I can't believe you let your friend talk to me that way," she says to Squealer. "Would it kill you to stand up for me for a change?"

Of course she takes it out on him.

Squealer doesn't say a word; he just looks down at the ground as the two of them walk away.

6

There is an hour and a half before you need to get to your internship, which means you have just enough time to get your food out of your hovercraft and have lunch with Babe. On the way to your hovercraft, a Warty waves at you. You don't recognize her but you wave back, only to realize too late, that she is waving at a Hogonian walking behind you. You try to play it off like you were just stretching, but you hear the two of them laughing as you continue on your way.

Way to go jackass. Make a fool out of yourself by waving at a total stranger.

You make it to your hovercraft and the inside feels like a furnace. Rummaging through the half empty drink bottles and food containers in the backseat, you find your lunch, open up the container, and sniff the inside. It doesn't smell too funky. You close the container and head toward the pond. Thankfully it is close to where you parked.

Babe is sitting under the willow tree next to the pond. She has a salad out, but she hasn't touched it; she is waiting for you to join her. You sit down next to her. A light breeze is blowing, the sun is shining, and white fluffy clouds float in the sky. It is a perfect day for a picnic.

"So what's a girl like you, doing in a place like this?" you ask her.

"Slumming it. Can you point me toward the nearest degenerate?" she asks while giving you a wink.

"You're in luck. Just last night, a girl told me that I am very bad boy."

"Oh, really? She sounds smart. I would like to meet her," Babe says. She gives you a kiss. "How has your day been?"

"It has been eventful. I got into a minor accident while heading to school, I almost died from boredom in my history class, and I dissected a head in my anatomy lab. You can guess how that turned out."

"Did Squealer vomit again?"

"Yeah, it was bad. The whole class watched and listened."

"Poor guy."

And that is why I love you.

"Wait, you said you got into an accident? What happened? Is everyone okay?" Babe asks.

Crap. Why did I mention that?

"For the most part. A human ran in front of my craft. Squealer and I are fine, but it died."

"Oh. I am glad you two are safe," she says while trailing off.

Babe opens up her salad, makes a fork with her nanosuit, and starts eating.

That could have gone worse.

You form a tentacle with your nanosuit. With it, you grab a pinky finger, dip it in the ranch, and throw it into your mouth. It tastes amazing, especially on your empty stomach. The finger is coated in a southwestern rub with a strong jalapeno flavor that mixes perfectly with the ranch and the natural taste of the pinky. Also, the bone in the center gives it a satisfying crunch.

"How has your day been?" you ask her.

"Not bad. I had my Psychology class today."

An awkward silence engulfs you two.

She didn't give me much to go on with that. She must be thinking about the human I ran over...

"So I noticed you are eating finger food today," she says.

Oh great.

"Yeah, my mom actually made my lunch today. I am pretty sure the world is coming to an end," you say. She smiles despite herself.

There is still hope.

"That was nice of her. I am not trying to nag you about this, but will you ever try vegetarianism with me? You know how I feel about what you eat."

"You know how I feel about what you eat. That isn't food, that is what food eats," you say while pointing at her salad. It is hard to suppress the frustration, especially after the day you have been having.

"Wilbur, a human died so that you can eat his fingers; just like a human died this morning under your hovercraft. How would you feel if your dad was killed so that a human could have a better tasting dinner? How would you feel if I was run over this morning?"

"I highly doubt a human was killed just for his fingers and I didn't intentionally run over that human this morning. It shouldn't have run in front of my craft."

"I know you didn't mean to do it, but a human died nonetheless," she says.

You have no response for her. The two of you continue to eat your lunches.

Why do girls always complain about things that can't be changed? It happened, let's move on.

A flock of Canadian geese make the mistake of landing on the pond. This pond is the only one on the planet that contains barbed toads, which have an affinity for birds. The founders transplanted the creatures from Hogart to remind them of their home planet and to prevent bird poop from littering their campus. Barbed toads are a dark grey color and are covered with curved spikes, including the tip of their tongues. Some of them can be as large as a human, but those tend to stay at the bottom of the pond.

The geese are oblivious of their impending doom, but you watch and wait. The first goose gets pulled under without a honk. A ripple and a few stray feathers remain in its place. The other geese are completely ignorant to their missing comrade and so is Babe. She seems to be lost in her own world.

The second goose rockets up into the sky from the impact of another toad's tongue. Instinctively, the goose stretches out its wings to feebly try to fly away, but the tongue is buried deep into its underbelly and the tips of spikes are poking out of the goose's stomach. The tongue retracts and pulls the goose down into the water. The goose vanishes within a second of impact, but its flock saw the whole ordeal. They begin to freak out and try to escape.

The next few seconds are filled with honking, blood, and death. One goose makes it off the water and starts to fly away as the rest of the flock are picked off by different toads. The flying goose is five meters above the water and almost completely past the pond, when the largest toad that you have ever seen bursts out of pond. It launches it tongue at the bird and snags the goose's foot. The tongue retracts and the goose is gobbled up. The goose's neck and head protrude out of the toad's mouth as the amphibian reenters the water. The goose's eyes stare at you just as it is taken into its final resting place.

That was awesome. That toad was even bigger than me.

"I hate those monsters. I can't believe they intentionally brought them here. How cruel is that?" Babe asks.

"Yeah ... it was definitely malicious of them."

"Don't act like you care. I know those toads are the only reason you want to have lunch here. You want to watch the show while we eat."

Her supernatural psychology powers are showing again. Too bad being pharmacy tech won't give me special powers.

"Okay, maybe that's true, but can't you see why the founders imported them here? The only things those birds do is poop on the grass."

"Your lack of respect for life is really disheartening. How can you possibly judge the value of those birds' lives by such brief glimpses?"

She is seriously defending the birds right now. What next, cockroaches?

"They were just some stupid birds. Just like this was just a stupid human," you say as you eat a thumb.

"That is a convenient argument when you

are the predator. How would you like it if Hogonians deemed us Pigians too stupid to appreciate our own lives and started eating us? "

"Humans are stupid, though. We were able to defeat them with ease. They also killed off most of the creatures on this planet. They obviously didn't respect life, so why should we give them that courtesy?"

"My argument isn't that intellect should be the deciding factor on whether a creature deserves to live or die. I am saying all creatures have the right to life. Some forfeit that right by the actions they take. The humans that caused the extinction of their native animals deserved the invasion, but the peaceful humans living today do not deserve to be harvested for their meat."

"So you are saying cockroaches deserve their lives and you are perfectly fine with them living in your house?"

"No, I am saying cockroaches in the wild deserve their lives and we shouldn't kill them meaninglessly. Cockroaches that invade my home forfeit their right to life by the choices they make. Respecting life doesn't mean you have to let all the other creatures walk all over you. It just means you should appreciate other creatures and their roles in the universe and that you should not destroy their lives for frivolous things, such as taste or entertainment. If I am starving to death and I encounter a human, I may kill and eat the human for survival without feeling guilty. On the other hoof, if I have plenty of plants to eat and I decide to kill the human anyways then I am in the wrong."

God, I love her, but sometimes she is just too kind. Defending inferior creatures is just ridiculous.

You finish eating the last of the finger food, but it doesn't taste nearly as good as before.

"What about divine command?" you ask.

"Divine command?"

"Yes. God told us that all the inferior creatures were ours to eat, including humans. You are telling me that God is wrong which is impossible."

"Who informed you that God said that? A Hogonian did. I can guarantee you humans also had a similar decree by God. I won't argue if God exists or not, but I am questioning the messenger who recorded the information. Maybe the messenger changed God's decree or maybe the original texts were translated wrong. We have no way of knowing for sure," Babe says

She is officially questioning the holy doctrines. It is a good thing Mom isn't here; otherwise, this conversation would be getting real nasty real quick.

"You know it isn't just about the humans. Cutting down on meat would be healthier for you and would help with your weight."

"What do you mean by that? I thought you liked my potbelly."

"I do like your potbelly. It is very rugged, but the extra weight does strain your heart. I don't want you to die of a heart attack at the age of thirty and be left a widow."

"That is very presumptuous of you to say that we will be married. What makes you think I would have you as my wife?" you ask cheekily.

"Oh whatever, I keep trying to get rid of you, but you won't leave me alone. You are like an orphaned human."

"It is good thing you like humans," you say just before giving her a kiss.

7

An alarm goes off shortly after the kiss. It is time to leave. Getting to the internship facility takes a few minutes and you have to go through the decontamination process, which consumes even more time.

"I have to head out."

"I know. I hope your internship goes well. Call me later if you have the time," Babe says.

"I will try. I love you. Have a good day."

"I love you too. Be safe."

You give Babe one last kiss and hug, and then you rush to your hovercraft. Hopping into the craft, you immediately turn on the autopilot. The autopilot takes you a different route than you normally go. It cuts through a neighborhood and saves you a couple of minutes.

You drive toward the entrance of the Nanoswine research facility. The perimeter of the facility is surrounded by a fence that is three stories high. Automated laser turrets line the top of the fence every few meters. Each gun is as big as you are and has multiple barrels, making it look similar to a Minigun. They are designed to destroy any vehicle or activist threatening the lab, but currently they are following your hovercraft's movement toward the gate. The first time you drove by the lab you thought it was a prison; Babe would still agree with that assessment.

The hovercraft stops outside the massive circular doors of the gate. An ancient guard steps out from his booth and hobbles toward your door. He is a Boaron with coarse grey hair and blackening tusks. The guard scans the hovercraft and you for the proper credentials. He also checks to make sure there are no stowaways or suspicious materials. The guard gives you a nod, slowly hobbles back to his booth, and opens the gate.

I hope the idiot who designed the gate security was fired. This is absolutely ridiculous. How do you automate everything except for the gate security?

After passing through the gate, you park your hovercraft and enter the main lobby of the facility. The floor of the lobby always amazes you. A cursorily glance of the floor gives you the impression that it is made of white marble, but a longer look reveals that the floor is always shifting and swirling. It is like you are walking over clouds, only the clicking of your hooves on the floor breaks the illusion. You still haven't discovered why they went with that design choice, but your best guess is that the architect really likes clouds.

You make your way toward the entrance of the labs. There are four Hogonians and two Boarons in line to go through the sterilization process. The labs are a clean zone, which means everyone must be sterilized before entering the testing areas to eliminate all foreign contaminants. You join the line and wait for your turn.

God, I hate this part. This is like waiting in line to be kicked in the nuts.

After a few minutes, it is finally your turn. You enter the sterilization chamber and the door seals behind you with a suction noise. You walk to the center of the room and stand on the two hoof marks. A scanning device, similar to what the gate guard had, scans your entire body.

"Welcome Wilbur," an automated voice says. "Your nanosuit will now be extracted and securely stored. It will be returned to you as soon as you leave the testing area."

Your nanosuit returns to its liquid mercury state and slides down your body into the receptacle below your hooves. You are left completely nude.

"The sterilization process will now begin.

It is recommended that you close your eyes to prevent irritation or other serious injury," the computer says.

You shut your eyes before the machine gets to the second sentence. Losing your eyesight is not on the agenda for today. Your ears start to hurt as the atmospheric pressure is lowered in the chamber. A metallic whining noise begins to resonate in front of you, followed by hurricane strength wind blowing across your body, almost knocking you over. After a few seconds, the wind stops, but the smell of lemons fills the chamber as a freezing cold liquid runs over your skin. The liquid is thicker than water and has slimy chunks in it. After a minute of the cold liquid, the hurricane strength wind returns, which dries your skin and then dies down. You can feel a soft powder landing on you. The powder starts to burn your skin, intensifying the longer it resides. You accidently inhale some of it, which immediately causes your nostrils to sting and your eyes to water.

I can't take this; it is too much. Why did I have to inhale that powder? I have never done that before.

You force a sneeze, which clears out some of the powder. The chamber showers another liquid, which relieves the horrible burning that was ravaging your skin. The relief is short lived, though. A mist sprays over you, freezing the surface of your body. It is followed by a high pitched flash that instantly removes the frost on your body and gives you the equivalent of a sunburn.

"Sterilization complete," the computer says.

Thank God.

The chamber gives you a customized nanosuit for your work day. Since you are only an intern, the capabilities of the nanosuit are limited to a guidance system of the facility, scanning, and note recordings. You feel crippled without the capabilities of your nanosuit.

You head toward your designated lab area. You work for Dr. Porkchop, one of the world's leading experts of nanotechnology. He is also a grade A asshole. He once fired a girl because she was pregnant and needed to go to the bathroom while a study was being conducted. Thankfully as an intern you seldom actually work with Dr. Porkchop. He is just the distant dictator that rules over every aspect of your internship.

There are many different research experiments being run by Dr. Porkchop. Babe would despise all of them if you actually told her about them. The one you are working on today focuses on what would happen if nanomites went rogue. At the start of the study, a milligram of rogue nanomites were unleashed on each test subject. Every day someone comes in and records the newest developments with the rogue nanomites. From the very first day of the experiment it was clear that rogue nanomites can be very dangerous, but you still have to extensively document what could happen if left untreated.

There are ten living test subjects left in this experiment. Each specimen is isolated in their own 3 meter by 3 meter chamber that is formed by an energy shield. If one of those energy shields failed while there were living nanomites still inside, the whole lab would automatically lock down and the contents would be purged through incineration. When you first watched the training video on your orientation day, you freaked out about that risk, but now you are completely numb to that danger. You imagine that is how islanders fill about living around an active volcano, up until it erupts and melts them with lava.

The first test subject has been infected for thirty days now. Initially there were no outward symptoms and the specimen felt fine. On day twelve, the human started to show signs of anemia. By day twenty-three, the nanomites were visible on the test subject's skin. They have been self replicating, mainly through harvesting the red blood cells' hemoglobin for iron. Today, you cannot see the human's skin. He is completely covered in nanomites. You go through the standard questionnaire with the specimen, acting like nothing out of the normal is happening. He is still able to answer but he has obviously lost all hope.

Specimens two through six have no visible symptoms, but the internal statistics are off the charts. They all have steeply elevated white blood cell counts as if they are fighting an infection. Specimens three, four, and six have extremely high blood pressure relative to their body size. Specimen five is starting to have kidney failure. Specimen two has developed schizophrenia.

Test subject seven is dead. An autopsy will need to be performed.

Specimen eight is a horror show. Like test subject one, the nanomites are harvesting the iron out of the human's hemoglobin to self replicate, but they are also eating the human's flesh; most likely to fuel continued operation. The human's head is half-eaten away where part of the skull is missing. You can see the brain pulsating as blood flow in and out. He is begging you to kill him as you ask the questionnaire.

This has to be one of the worst internships in the world.

Specimens nine and ten have no symptoms. Their nanomites appear to have died off. As you finish up your notes, one of Dr. Porkchops assistants walks into the room. She is a short Hogonian with a pudgy snout. You can never remember her name and her online profile is blocked.

"Good timing. Dr. Porkchop needs you to join an expedition to capture more test subjects," she says.

"Capture more test subjects?"

"Yes, the lab has a new experiment that is testing the heat shielding of a prototype paneling. The result is a lot of toasted humans and a need for new specimens."

"Don't you have a standard crew that captures new humans?"

"Of course we do, but one of them called in sick and you are the only expendable asset onsite. Head to the landing bay as soon as you are done here," she says and walks out before you can say another word.

God, I hope she meant my time was expendable, not my life.

You finish your notes and start for the landing bay. As you walk by specimen eight's cell, you notice he is lying in the corner and no longer screaming. His suffering may have finally ended. You exit the testing area.

8

Through the use of your nanosuit's navigation system, you find the landing bay without much issue. There are over two dozen aircrafts parked in the bay, but most of them are personal vehicles. At the very far end of the room are the company vehicles, two shuttles and an interceptor. As you walk toward the back, you spot a speeder that costs at least ten million credits.

Oh my God, that speeder is calling my name. It is a shame that I would have to sell all my organs to afford the down payment.

As you get closer to the shuttles, the interceptor captures your attention. It is sleek and thin with very large cannons on the front. The cabin can only sit one person in it, but the vehicle looks very fast and powerful. It wouldn't do well attacking a heavily armored vehicle, but with the proper hit and run tactics, it could take on any vehicle found on Earth. Once you are within a few meters, you can start to see a layer of dust on it. It hasn't been used in quite awhile.

The shuttles are the exact opposite of the interceptor. It is like the engineer was trying for the least aerodynamic vehicle in existence. The main body of the vehicle is large and rectangular. It has massive wings with even bigger turbines on them, but the vehicle must be slow and clumsy. From the outside, it looks like the shuttle can contain at least eighty people. The surface of the shuttle is dinged up with patches of different metals covering some of the holes, while other holes are left gaping.

Standing outside of the shuttle is a Boaron, a Hogonian, and a Warty. The Boaron is tall, muscular, and about twenty years older than you. He has long white tusks and his nanosuit looks like silver battle armor. The Hogonian is slightly older than you and is about your size. Her nanosuit design screams scientist, but she is a very pretty one. The Warty is half your size and has long grey hair covering his whole body. His nanosuit makes your eyes hurt with the weird patterns covering it.

"You must be our fill in," the Boaron says.

"Yes, my name is Wilbur, nice to meet you."

"My name is Hoover. I will be leading this expedition. The midget over here is named Pumba. He is our token Warty scientist. And this lovely sow is Petunia, our lead primatologist on this trip. Let's get on board. We are already way behind schedule," says the Boaron.

You walk up the ramp to the main entrance. The interior of the shuttle is smaller than you thought it would be. Hoover barely has clearance for his head. Most of the shuttle must be below this room. There are openings running the length of the room on both sides of the shuttle. In the middle of each opening is a turret that is as tall as you are with a crank and either a spear or harpoon in the barrel of the gun.

"This is where you will spend the entire expedition. Be mindful of the two openings. If you fall out, we will have to notify your next of kin," Hoover says.

Note to self: don't fall out.

"Ziffel, let's head out," Hoover tells the pilot.

The turbines start up. They make a low humming noise, which is surprising considering their size. The shuttle lifts off and leaves the bay. You brace yourself against the wall to avoid falling out.

"Have you ever been reeling before?" Hoover asks.

"No, but it looks like a good time. My dad always wanted to take me but it never worked out."

The shuttle is heading toward the Chicago Barrier. At the pace the aircraft is going, it will only take a few minutes. You look below; the vehicles are the size of toys.

Wow, we truly are small in the grand scale of things.

"You have not lived before today, my friend. There is nothing like it on this planet. Just remember to aim for the torso."

"The torso? Why the torso?"

"The torso is the biggest target on a human and the sturdiest. If you shoot one in an arm or leg, there is a large chance that the limb will rip off and you lose your prey. For our purposes, shooting them in the head is also not an option because it will most likely die."

"Sounds like you have been doing this a lot."

"Oh yeah, I use to go reeling every weekend with my old boar, before I started to get paid to do it. We preferred to go to Detroit, though. They put up a better fight up there."

The shuttle is almost to the Chicago Barrier now. At this proximity, the top of the barrier is too tall to be seen, even from thirty stories in the air.

Hard to believe that this is the same structure that I see every day from home. That tiny snow globe is a lot more intimidating from here.

"We are about to go through the barrier. Please brace yourselves. There will be turbulence," the pilot says.

Seconds before impacting the Chicago

Barrier, the pilot turns on a barrier around the shuttle with the same frequency as the giant one. As the two barriers touch, they meld together, shaking furiously in the process. The shaking stops abruptly once the joining completes and the barrier in front of the shuttle has vanished.

Thank God.

Within the barrier, you realize the skyscrapers are still a ways off. Below the shuttle are some decrepit low level buildings, grassy fields, and a road filled with abandoned vehicles. Many of the vehicles had crashed into one another, probably from when the EMG blast disabled them while still in use.

"This is not what I expected. I thought it would be completely filled with skyscrapers."

"No, the Hogonians optimized it to capture the largest amount of humans while minimizing cost, so they included some of the suburbs outside of the main city structures. They also included a large section of the lake, so that the humans can somewhat self-sustain," says Petunia.

As the shuttle flies closer to the main city, the buildings below start to grow in size and frequency. Most of the buildings have not been well maintained, which give you an eerie vibe. It makes sense considering that the humans can't get supplies from the outside world, but you never thought about how the windows would break and the walls would degrade. Some of the buildings have obviously been scrapped for supplies to maintain the other structures, but even the ones that have been maintained do not compare to the buildings outside of the barrier.

"What is up with all the blast marks and bullet holes in some of these buildings? Is it from the initial invasion?" you ask.

"Yeah, most of that is from the early years of the invasion. They would fight amongst themselves over territory disputes or try to take down any shuttles in the area. It has been years since any of them have had mechanized projectile weapons, considering they lack the resources to use or maintain them. Every once in awhile we spot one with a bow or slingshot, but they are taken care of swiftly."

The shuttle is now surrounded by towering skyscrapers, but you still don't see any human activity down on the streets. Every once in awhile you notice movement behind some of the broken windows in the buildings, but you can never make out what was causing it. It is like you are flying through a ghost town.

"So where are all the humans?"

"They're hiding inside the buildings and in the underground tunnels. They don't trust any flying vehicles anymore," says Hoover.

A large cylindrical building has toppled over in the street in front of the shuttle. It is leaning against another skyscraper and dangling over the street. Below the toppled building is a pile of human vehicles. As the shuttle gets closer, you can see that there are hundreds of those vehicles still in that building, which must have been some sort of pre-invasion garage. Instead of flying over the toppled building, the pilot decides to go under.

Oh crap, this is it. I am going to die during my internship. Isn't that a pathetic thought?

As the shuttle flies under the building, you imagine one of those vehicles coming crashing down upon the shuttle or even worse yet, the building finally collapsing to the ground. Your vehicle makes it through without issue, but your heart feels like it is ready to explode.

"Ziffel, next time please fly over the toppled building. I want to die of stroke while having sex at the age of 180, not by being crushed to death by a falling building. Thanks," Hoover says.

"Will do boss. Are you hoping to have better luck getting some when you are 180 or will you be paying for your last ride?" Ziffel asks.

"As long as your mom is still around, I should do just fine," Hoover says. "This looks like a good spot. Let's start attracting some humans. Deploy the chicken."

Deploy the chicken? What does that mean? Are they messing with me?

A mechanical grinding noise starts below where you are standing. A chicken drops from

the shuttle. It falls thirty stories and smacks
down on the pavement without a hint of
bouncing. Dozens more start falling from the
shuttle.

"You know, when I woke up this
morning; it never crossed my mind that I would
take part in raining down chicken from a
shuttle."

"We will try not to hold your lack of
imagination against you," Pumba says.

"I appreciate that. There is a point to this,
right? We are not doing this just for shits and
giggles?"

"Nope, we just do it because it is fun. We
are going cow tipping next. Yes, there is a
reason for this. Watch the humans," Hoover
says.

A few humans are approaching the fallen
chickens now. All of them are approaching
slowly and looking up at the shuttle. None of
them look like they trust the situation.

"Oh, ok, so we are using the chicken to
get the humans out in the open?"

"Yeah, it's called chicken chumming.
They say the first attempts were done with
frozen chicken. It didn't work out so well. The
chickens would shatter when they hit the
ground and the humans were too afraid of being
hit by one to come near the drop zone," Petunia
says.

"Why would they fall for this? If I was a

human and saw chickens falling from a shuttle, I would not feel compelled to get closer; no matter how hungry I was."

"Humans are stupid. Isn't that reason enough?" Hoover asks.

"I guess. What do we do now?"

"Now is the fun part. Aim your Jolter at the nearest human and press the trigger to fire. If you hit your target, you can reel it in by turning the grip on the right side of your Jolter or by pressing and holding the trigger. It is a much more visceral and enjoyable experience to actually reel in your prey; but, if you have the strength of a piglet, you may require the motorized trigger. Be prepared for constant ridicule from us, if you do use the trigger."

Hoover is referring to the turret that is next to you. You step behind it and aim the Jolter toward the ground. The device has a large crosshair at the top, which makes aiming easy.

Please let me be good at this.

You aim the Jolter at the closest human and fire. A metal harpoon, about the size of your snout, shoots down toward your target with a thin cord attached to it. Just as the harpoon is about to collide with the human, he bends down to pick up a chicken and your shot buzzes over his head. The harpoon clashes into the cracked asphalt behind the man and a blue spark bursts out from the impact. All the nearby humans flee the scene. A few of them try to throw rocks at the ship during their retreat.

"Crap. Sorry guys."

"That wasn't bad for your first attempt. Your timing was just off. Next time, wait for the human to pick up the chicken before firing. Ziffel, let's move it over a couple blocks and try again," Hoover yells to the pilot.

The shuttle blasts forward, flying three blocks down the road from the last sight. As the vehicle flies through a back alley to the right, you notice a wrecked shuttle scattered across the ground. The whole left side of the downed ship is torn to pieces as if a giant missile had taken it down. There are skeletons lying around the debris, which are unmistakably that of Boarons.

Yeah, this is safe. I would have been better off just doing the regular routine at the lab. They said that the humans were out of projectile weapons, but what if they have other means of taking down vehicles? It wouldn't be hard to setup wires between buildings to snag flying crafts, like a spider catching flies; only in this instance the fly would explode or crash land into the pavement.

After a few more turns, the shuttle hovers over a new target area. To the south is a river with dark brown water, which smells like death, while to the north is a building that looks like it was just built. There are columns scattered along the river bank, one of which has a bronze figure of a human head. Directly below the shuttle is another bronze head, which is smashed through the windshield of a minivan that has a skeleton sitting in the driver seat. Like before, there are no living humans on the street, but the look of the building to the north is definitely encouraging.

"Okay, this time I will be using the other Jolter. With two of us at work, we should have some luck this round. If you do snag one, make sure you start reeling it up right away. The other humans may try to intervene if they can reach your snagged target," says Hoover.

The shuttle starts dropping chickens and a few humans enter the street. A child and an old man are in the perfect position for you, but you decide to wait for a better target. The risk of killing one of those humans is too high to merit a shot. Then you hear Hoover's Jolter fire, followed by a brief high-pitched scream down below.

"I got one," yells Hoover as he rapidly cranks the Jolter.

You run to the other side of the shuttle and look down below. Hoover shot a female human in the back. Her unconscious body dangles at the end of the wire like a marionette as she gets pulled up toward the ship.

The sound of cabinets being opened and closed brings your attention back into the shuttle. Pumba comes out of the back holding some sort of collar, while Petunia gets closer to the opening. You return to your original spot to avoid getting in the way. Hoovers face is strained as he reels in the human. Once the human gets close enough to the opening, Petunia pulls the human inside and sets her on the deck. Pumba places the collar on the human while Hoover pulls the harpoon out of the girl's back and sprays some sort of foam into the hole.

"What is up with that collar and the foam?" you ask Hoover.

"The collar keeps the human unconscious by supplying a constant sedative. The foam is to sanitize and clot the wound," replies Hoover. Hoover finds a sharpened piece of metal on the human and throws it out of the shuttle. "Once all weapons are removed from the human, we can place the test subject in the holding cell." The floor opens up below the human, dropping her directly into the holding cell.

The next hour continues with Hoover snagging the humans and everyone preparing the new test subjects for holding. You don't have much of a chance of snagging your own, considering how fast Hoover is at this job, but you are close on a few occasions. One time you shoot the chicken that your target is holding, resulting in a nasty shock for that human and a ton of laughter up in the shuttle.

"Okay, Chicken Jolter, we have to head back in thirty minutes, so you better step up your game if you want to reel in your first human," Hoover says to you.

"I don't know; I was thinking about sticking with the chickens. There a much smaller target to hit."

I am not leaving here empty hoofed. Dr. Porkchop will never let me go reeling again, if I do. This may be a little dangerous, but it is also way more entertaining than my normal lab work.

"Chicken Jolter, shoot the one with the backpack. Hoover hold up on firing. We have a target for our research," Pumba says.

Hoover steps away from his Jolter and joins your side of the shuttle. You see the teenager with a backpack standing over a chicken. You aim at his chest and take a deep breath. As he squats down to pick up the poultry, you fire the Jolter. The harpoon blasts out of the barrel and launches toward your target. You forgot to factor in the wind, but the harpoon still hits him in the shoulder. The human shakes violently and drops to the ground as the electricity courses through his body. You start cranking the reel. It is a lot harder than it looked.

"Not bad," says Hoover.

"Good work. Get him on up here," says Pumba.

After two minutes of reeling, your arm feels like it is on fire and you are out of breath, but you are able to get the human within reach, without looking like a piglet. Pumba brings the teenager into the shuttle, Hoover puts a collar on him, and Petunia takes off his backpack. You sit down to recuperate.

The teenager is a Hispanic male with short black hair. He has tiny ears, a petite nose, and lips that are almost nonexistent, but his eyebrow hair more than makes up for it. He has the largest unibrow that you have ever seen with absolutely no hint of a divide between the two brows. He is wearing a hodgepodge of different cloths with different colors stitched together into a garment that looks as if he took a quilt and cut holes for his head and arms.

"So what is this research?" you ask.

"We are collecting information on the habits of humans in Chicago. Some basic information is easy to gather, but carrying bags are rare and provide a wealth of otherwise unobtainable data." Petunia says as she dumps the contents of the backpack onto the floor.

You have your nanosuit analyze the different items. Most of the items are what you would expect to see on a human. Like other humans captured today, there are some sharp pieces of metal that would be used as weapons or tools. There are also water containers and food supplies scattered on the floor. The rat jerky and seasoned cockroaches are particularly gross. Unexpectedly, there are some tattered books and papers, including: George Orwell's *Animal Farm*, Jonathan Swift's *A Modest Proposal*, and Stephen King's *Under the Dome*.

"Were you expecting to see books on him?" you ask.

"Yeah, it is more common than what you would think. It makes sense though, considering they are trapped in here without electricity. They need some sort of entertainment besides breeding and rat fighting," Pumba says with a chuckle.

"Between those options, give me rat fighting, any day," you say returning the chuckle.

A few more minutes pass as they gather data. The shuttle moves to another site, this time not over a street but a park. The ground is made of broken tan tiles. Lying on top of the tiles are shards of steel, parts of which look polished, but the majority of it is covered in grime.

The shuttle starts dropping chickens as your human is placed in containment and his belongings are stored away. A group of humans approach the bait, not a crowd of random people, but an organized group. Everyone else seems calm, but you are getting nervous.

Do they see this often?

"Wilbur, take a break. I am going to capture one of these," says Hoover. He looks very serious as if this one is personal. He aims the Jolter and waits. Only a few of the humans below are interested in the chickens, most are staring directly up at the shuttle. They know.

Hoover fires. The harpoon hits the tallest

and most muscular brute in the chest. Hoover starts reeling him up as soon as he snags his target. The group tries to grab hold of the man, but Hoover is cranking him up fast enough where the human slips out of their grasp. The brute is halfway to the shuttle when the convulsing from the electricity stops. He dangles unconsciously as Hoover gets the man to the opening.

Petunia catches the brute's leg, pulls him into the shuttle, and sets him on the floor. As Pumba tries to put the collar on the human, his eyes open up. The human was always conscious! The brute punches Pumba in the chest, sending him tumbling into the back of the shuttle, and stands up. The man pulls out a sharpened piece of metal that is the size of his forearm, as Petunia and Hoover start to realize what is happening. You pull Petunia away from the brute, as the human slashes with the shard. The metal misses her throat by a centimeter. Hoover kicks the man in the chest, but it doesn't faze him. The human slashes Hoover's shoulder causing a horrific metallic screeching noise as the shard scrapes across Hoover's nanosuit. You grab your Jolter and try to turn it toward the attacker, but it can't turn that far inside. The brute lunges at Hoover with the shard, when Petunia kicks him in the side, sending him flying out of the shuttle. The cord of the Jolter rapidly unravels as the human falls. Hoover forms a blade with his nanosuit and slashes the cord. The brute drops twenty stories and lands head first onto the broken tiles. The splattered body on the ground looks like that of a bug on a windshield.

"Holy shit," exclaims Petunia.

"That is enough excitement for one day. Ziffel get us back to the lab," says Hoover.

Pumba hobbles back into the main area of the shuttle. He is a bit bruised but doesn't look seriously injured. Petunia and Hoover are sitting down, trying to settle their nerves. Your heart feels likes it is ready to explode.

"Have you ever seen that before?" you ask while trying not to sound too freaked out.

"Yeah, it is rare, but it does happen. Sometimes the electricity isn't strong enough to knock out the bigger targets. They are normally not that crafty, though," says Hoover as if his life wasn't in jeopardy a few second ago.

"Have you encountered those humans before?"

"We go after that gang on every expedition. They are one of the main forces in Chicago. We try to dwindle the corruptive elements so that the rest of the population is not tainted."

The rest of the flight is filled with silence. Everyone is lost in their own thoughts.

If Babe had endured that attack like I did, her stance on human rights would be completely different. I bet she would be more than willing to cook up some man after one of them tried to kill her.

The shuttle passes through the barrier, but you don't pay attention to it. The brute's attack is the only thing that matters right now.

Screw them. They are vicious and deserve to be eaten. I can't believe Babe wants them protected. It is completely ridiculous.

"Good work today, Wilbur. I will make sure Dr. Porkchop finds out how big of an asset you were," says Hoover.

"Thanks. I appreciate it. Today was definitely interesting."

The shuttle lands in the lab. Hoover and Pumba jump out. Petunia stays back. From the look on her face, something is definitely on her mind. Petunia gives you a hug. You are completely flabbergasted.

Where did that come from?

"Thank you for saving my life," she says.

"Thank you for saving mine. If you hadn't kicked that brute out of the shuttle, we would have all died," you say.

Petunia gives you a smile and jumps down.

What a day.

9

You look at the time. You have three minutes to get to the restaurant. Mom is going to kill you. Rushing through the exterior containment sequence, you put on your nanosuit and run to your hovercraft. The autopilot starts driving you to the restaurant while you try to catch your breath. Running is a very rare occurrence for you, which is exactly how you like it.

After settling down, you turn on the broadcasts of streaming video. The whole interior cabin is replaced by a Warty sitting next to a female human. The Warty has a hoof over her shoulder and she looks completely repulsed. Below the pair is a caption: Humaniality: Warty marries human.

"Don't judge us. We can't help it. It is true love. We were meant for either and being different species can't stop it," the Warty says.

Wow, that is just gross.

You change the station. It is some soap opera. From what you can tell, a Hogonian girl is vehemently upset because she unknowingly slept with her boyfriend's evil twin brother and now she is pregnant and doesn't know which one is the father. For some reason there is also a Boaron ghost following her around.

So is that her dead husband or her dead dad? This show makes no sense.

You change the station again. A song with the pace of a turtle and the tone of a funeral is playing. An image of an emaciated human child playing in a filthy stream appears. It transitions to an image of a hovercraft accident where a human went through the windshield of the craft and the female Pigian driver died. A Hogonian doctor appears.

"Please spay or neuter your human and prevent tragedies like these from happening," the doctor says.

I doubt Spike would like that much. First we snip his vocal cords then we snip his testicles.

The restaurant is now within sight. It has a large animated sign that shows two dead humans hanging upside down on hooks with x's for eyes, while a third human repeatedly gets his head chopped off by a butcher's cleaver. Below the animation, flashes the name of the restaurant, The Slaughterhouse, in neon red letters which looks like blood spewing out of the decapitated body of the human.

I bet Babe loves that sign. I completely forgot they had that.

After parking, you rush inside. There is a massive line of people waiting to be seated, but you don't see Mom or Dad. You work your way through the crowd toward the registration desk. Many of the people in line give you a dirty look, especially this one Warty mother who is holding her ugly piglet against her shoulder.

"Can I help you?" the greeter asks.

"Actually, I just spotted my parents. Thanks, though."

Making your way into the restaurant, you head toward your parents table. Interior design is not one of your favorite past times, but this restaurant's atmosphere draws your attention. The walls are a dark blood red with chrome lighting fixtures placed over each table. Scattered along the walls are mounted brute heads, each one with a different look or expression.

As you approach the table, you notice Mom and Dad already have drinks. Dad is working on his second beer while Mom has sweet tea. Dad looks exhausted. It must have been another hard day for him. Mom is talking his ear off, complaining about how conniving one of the nurses is. Dad is obviously zoning her out. Mom notices you walking toward the table.

"Look who finally decided to show up,"

she says.

"Sorry, my internship ran long. Happy birthday Dad."

"How exactly does that happen? It took extra long to write down notes about another meaningless study?"

"One of the shuttle crew members called in sick today, so I joined them on a reeling trip. I even caught one," you say.

"That is great. I wish I could have been there with you. Was it a brute?" Dad asks.

"No, it was a teenager. The very last one we caught was a brute. It nearly killed us. We ended up kicking it out of the shuttle and it splattered on the ground like a rotten pumpkin."

"Maybe you should stick to the meaningless notes," Mom says. She looks really worried.

"Nonsense, our Wilbur is finally growing up. The world is a dangerous place and he just showed it who the boss is."

A waiter comes up to your table.

"Can I get you something to drink?" he asks.

"Water please," you reply.

You start looking over the menu. The hors d'oeuvres section mostly contains items that you can see at any restaurant, except for the grey matter gumbo, the coconut lady fingers and the stuffed cojones. The grey matter gumbo is a stew made with real man brains, okra, and green peppers. It is served in the skull of the human. The coconut lady fingers are fingers encrusted in a coconut breading and comes with a lime dipping sauce. The stuffed cojones are Mexican testicles stuffed with cream cheese and diced jalapenos.

I guess I will pass on the appetizers, considering that eating a stew out of a human's head doesn't sound good after my lab today, I already had finger food for lunch, and I will never be in the mood for man balls.

Continuing down the menu, you see the salad section and don't even give it a cursorily glance. They have large feline and canine sections, but you had dog yesterday and you're not really a cat person, so you skip over them as well. You are left with the entree section and desserts.

Sorry, Babe. No salad tonight. Not after that Brute attack. Maybe tomorrow I will pass on the meat.

"What are you guys getting?" you ask.

"I am going to get the feline cutlets," Mom replies.

"Baby back ribs," Dad says.

Baby back ribs do sound good, but that isn't a lot of meat. Plus their barbecue sauce is too sweet. I could get the roast man, but that would feed five and it is very expensive. Ooh, they do have charred toddler and you get to pick out the one you want. That really sounds good, even though, I always get that from here. Let's see what their current selection is.

You have your nanosuit connect with the live feed of the toddler cam. There are fifteen kids playing in an indoor playground, which has a seesaw, a slide, a set of monkey bars, and a set of swings. The walls of the room are painted to look as if the playground is located outside, surrounded by beautiful rolling green hills and a blue sky filled with white clouds and a bright yellow sun. Most of the children seem to be enjoying themselves, except for a boy crying in the corner and a girl who was just pushed off the seesaw.

As you focus on the different toddlers, your nanosuit shows the statistics for the kids including weight, height, age, muscle percentage, fat percentage, and cost in credits. You look for the most appetizing one and keep coming back to the bully who pushed the little girl. He is a bit expensive, 85 credits, but he has a high body fat percentage that will make him delicious and a personality that merits being eaten.

"Are you going to get the charred toddler again?" Mom asks.

"It is my favorite thing here and they just so happen to have a little brat that deserves to be eaten."

The waiter comes back to the table with your water. He asks, "Are you ready to order or do you still need a few minutes?"

"We are ready to order," Dad says. "I will have the baby back ribs with mashed potatoes as the side."

"I will have the feline cutlets with a side of steamed broccoli," Mom says.

"Certainly, and you?" he asks while looking in your direction.

"I would like the charred toddler, rare. Particularly, I want number 42."

"Gordy, please extract number 42," the waiter says to someone in the back. "That comes with an onion blossom and fresh greens. Would you like to add a side for ten credits?"

"No thanks."

"Okay, I will be back shortly with some fresh biscuits. If you need anything, please don't hesitate to ask," the waiter says. He walks away as you take a sip of water. This restaurant is one of the few that still employs waiters. Most have the process completely automated, which your parents do not like.

You are still watching the toddler cam. Number 42 kicks a little boy half his size. The little kid screams like he is dying, causing his face to turn red. All the other kids are staying there distance while watching the commotion play out. The bully is so focused on the screaming kid that he doesn't notice the giant claw coming down above him. The claw is around his head before he realizes there is something wrong. It looks like a giant version of the crane game that some arcades use to have, only in this instance the stuffed animal kicks and screams as the crane grabs hold of it and pulls it out of the box. You disconnect from the feed.

"So Wilbur, are you any closer in figuring out what you want to do when you graduate?" Mom asks.

"Not really. I will most likely move off this planet, but besides that, I have no clue."

"You're still thinking about moving away?"

"Yeah, this planet isn't meant for a Pigian. I will never get ahead in life on a world controlled by Boarons. I need to be on a planet ruled by my own kind who will accept me as an equal."

"That is ridiculous. Earth is perfectly fine planet for us. You are just being paranoid," Mom says.

"No, he isn't," Dad says while staring at his beer. "How can you possibly say that after thirty-six years on this planet? Have you completely forgotten about how life was on Pigopia? We are treated like second class citizens here. For God's sake, it took us five years to get a loan for the house. Five years. I guarantee you, if we were Boarons that would have never taken that long."

"You are doing it again. You're brainwashing Wilbur with your anti-Boaron sentiments and now he is actually thinking about moving away because of you," Mom scolds.

Both your parents quiet down as the waiter comes back. He has the promised biscuits. The smell is intoxicating. Your mouth salivates. He sets them on the table and you try not to snatch them up too hastily. You wait two seconds, which is an eternity considering the current circumstances, and grab one of the biscuits. The buttery, cheesy goodness touches your taste buds and all is well in the universe.

"Your food should be out shortly," he says and walks to the adjacent table. A Hogonian at that table looks very familiar. You try to look her up online, but her profile is private. She is completely transfixed on her date.

Who is that girl and where do I know her from?

Sadly, you finish your biscuit and at high class restaurants like this one, they only bring one complimentary item per person.

"He has the right idea, though. Trying to find a job here will be almost impossible, but there will be opportunities on other planets," Dad says.

"I can't believe you. That is completely untrue. There are plenty of opportunities here," Mom says.

"Not for a Pigian in his field, everyone

will be looking for a Hogonian. He could find a job cleaning tables or picking up trash without issue. Or he could join the family business and exterminate cockroaches for the rest of his life. Those are his 'opportunities' here," Dad says. He takes a long sip of his beer.

This is going to bug me all night if I don't figure it out. I have seen her before, but we are not friends online. Is she in one of my classes?

"Just because you couldn't make anything of your life on this planet, doesn't mean our son will do the same."

"Oh, so it is my fault that I am only an exterminator?"

"Who else would it be?"

"How about the damn Boarons who didn't hire me as a manager because of my species? How about them for starters?" Dad says in a raised voice. Some "ignorant folks" may even call it a yell.

Oh great, they're fighting about this again and they are completely oblivious to their current surroundings. What a lovely birthday dinner…

"That was thirty years ago. Why didn't you apply for any other jobs since then? Oh wait, I know, because you gave up, which makes it your own fault," Mom says.

The Hogonian girl is now staring at your table, but she isn't looking at your fighting parents, she is looking at you. Her eyebrows are scrunched and her lips are pursed as if the clockworks in her head are straining to figure something out and are pulling the muscles in her face to make the calculations. She snaps her face back toward her boyfriend, once she realizes that you are also looking back at her.

She definitely recognizes me, but that doesn't narrow down where I know her from.

Your parents continue to fight. You keep your mouth shut. It is an old song and dance, one that will get you kicked if you get in the middle.

The food better get here soon. They are on the verge of ripping each other's throats out.

"Maybe my mother was right about you. Maybe I should have ended up with Hampton. He ended up being a cardiac surgeon," Mom says.

"I would love to see that one. Then you would get those mysterious bruises and black eyes that magically appear out of nowhere like his current wife does," Dad says.

The two of them finally stop arguing.

The waiter brings your table's order with the help of another server. The baby back ribs look cooked to perfection. The feline cutlets don't look appetizing, although they are breaded and fried. Your order takes up a whole serving tray. The charred toddler is on a bed of greens over a silver platter that has ornamental piglets with wings around the rim of the dish. The skin is cooked to a golden-red. Its hair has been shaved off and replaced by an onion blossom on top of its head. Cucumber slices are in place of its eyes. Radishes are in its ears and an apple is stuffed in its mouth.

With your nanosuit, you form a knife at the end of one hoof and a fork on the other. You shove the fork into the toddler's side and cut with the knife. The meat is white, maybe a hint of pink.

"How is everything?" the waiter asks.

"I asked for mine rare, but this ..." You show him the only slight pink meat. " is definitely not rare."

"Oh, I am sorry, sir. Let me talk to my manager and see what we can do for you."

"Thanks," you say while your parents give you a dirty look. The waiter walks off with your overcooked meal. "What?"

"Do you have to make a scene?" Mom asks.

That is funny. I am the one making the scene.

"I am not making a scene. We are paying good money for this meal. I asked for it rare and that was definitely not rare."

A Boaron dressed in a tuxedo approaches the table. His tusks are very predominant and fit well with the broadness of his snout.

Of course the manager is a Boaron. I don't see a single Pigian working here. They probably have one of us washing dishes in the back, though. Pigians aren't elegant enough to work with customers in such an establishment, but they are good enough for menial chores.

"Sir, I am deeply sorry about the overcooking of your order. If you would like, you can pick another toddler and we will prepare it to your specifications; or we have Irish veal available that is not on the menu. All at no charge, of course." The last sentence seems to cause him physical pain as he speaks it.

"How old is the Irish veal?"

Mom shoots you an exasperated look. Dad shakes his head with a smirk. He enjoys the discomfort of the manager too.

"It is aged to perfection at 8 months old and the only one we have left."

"It sounds delicious. I will take it. Please make sure it is rare, though."

"Certainly, would you prefer a C-section or induced labor to prepare it? A C-section will be faster, but induced labor tends to bring out the flavor."

"C-section."

This dinner has already taken way too long.

"Will do. It will be out shortly," says the manager. He gives you a slight bow and walks away.

The Hogonian girl and her date now have their food. They both ordered salads and seem to be enjoying them. Well, the girl is. The guy drowned his salad in ranch and takes quick bites with long pauses in between them.

Who orders a salad at The Slaughterhouse? That is sacrilegious.

"Well, Wilbur?" Mom asks.

"What?"

"I asked if Babe will move off planet with you after you both graduate. Have you even brought it up with her?"

"We have talked about it, but nothing is set in stone. It is a rather big decision to make and there is still plenty of time to make it."

Plus there is the whole meat issue.

"It is approaching faster than you think. It feels like just yesterday you were my little piglet in my hooves. Now you are talking about moving to a different planet far from me."

"Mom, I am not planning on moving to a different planet just to get away from you. I am trying to find the best opportunities for success and Earth isn't it. I wish it was."

This dinner just keeps getting worse and worse. Next thing I know, Babe will walk through the door, kick me in the nuts, and then break up with me.

"Wilbur, it will be hard for your mother to see you go, if you do move off planet, but you have to make the right choice for yourself. We will try to support you no matter which way you go," Dad says.

"Thanks."

The waiter comes back with the Irish veal. On the plate is an eight month human fetus covered in gravy and surrounded by chunks of potatoes and carrots. It smells better than your grandma's stew. You cut out a chunk of the arm and the meat is a dark red.

"Thank you, it looks great. What type of gravy is that?" you ask.

"It is a special amniotic gravy invented by our chefs. Please let me know if you need anything else," the waiter says as he walks away.

He definitely seemed sincere by walking away before I could even respond.

"If that thing was any rarer, it would cry," Dad says.

"Just the way I like it."

You take a bite. It is perfection. All of your inhibitions, caused by the dissection earlier and Babe's speech, wash away. You give into the flavor and ravenously eat your meal. The hands are the best part, even though, one of the fingernails gets stuck between your teeth and the bones are not nearly as crunchy as mature finger food. By the end, not a single piece of meat, chunk of potato, nor stray carrot escape your stomach.

"I guess you liked it," Mom says.

"It is my new favorite food. I thought I knew how good meat could be, but I was dead wrong."

Your mom just shakes her head.

The salad eaters have paid for their meal

and are walking toward the front. They seem to be rushing out. As they pass your table, the girl glares at you as if she wants to take a knife and stab you in the gut.

What is up with that?

"They didn't look too happy," Mom says.

"Yeah, did you notice the look she gave me?"

"No, I didn't. You are just being paranoid again."

The waiter comes back to the table.

"Would anyone like dessert?"

"No thanks. We are ready to checkout," Mom says.

"Well, thank you for joining us this evening. We look forward to seeing you next time," the waiter says and walks away.

I doubt that.

"So what are we doing for the rest of your birthday?" you ask Dad.

"Chores. I am going to try to eliminate the squatters tonight. Then I am going to get some sleep. It has been a long day."

"Not exactly the most thrilling birthday. What made it a long day?"

"I had to deal with a toxic shrew infestation today. They shoot a foul smelling acid out of their crotch that can burn through standard nanosuits, which means during my whole day I had to wear a protective suit that was as hot as a dragon's asshole."

"They shoot acid out of their crotch? That is messed up."

"It is a defense mechanism. I've seen some of their natural predators from Bor. They would have been extinct a long time ago without that acid."

"That is pretty impressive that they got all the way to Earth."

"Yeah, we think the little bastards stowed away on one of the military transports. By the time we were contacted, there were hundreds of them scurrying in the basement and throughout the walls. You should have seen the floor of the basement. It was a warzone. There were layers of…"

"This isn't an appropriate conversation to have at a restaurant," Mom interrupts.

Dad stares at her for a few seconds with a blank expression.

"Let's get out of here so the civilized folk can enjoy their dinner without having to hear about my daily job," he says. He finishes off the last of his beer and stands up. Mom and you follow suit.

On the way toward the door, Dad loudly says, "So like I was saying, there was a layer of shit on the ground that was at least as deep as my hooves."

Mom shakes her head. Many of the "civilized folk" are completely outraged by the passing conversation, particularly your waiter and an elderly lady who is wearing way too much perfume.

I bet she regrets interrupting him like that now.

"The shrews didn't mind though. There were multiple nests made out of crap. The babies rolled around in it while the parents humped each other without shame." He glares back at Mom during the last part.

"How did you end up getting rid of them?"

"After assessing the situation, we setup a barrier around the building then gassed the place. It was the only way to ensure we killed them all. They also paid for cleanup, so we had to remove all the corpses and most of the shit. The building still has scorch marks from where the acid hit, though. Good luck cleaning that up without completely replacing the material."

"Do you feel bad that you had to kill the babies? They really didn't cause any harm."

I really should have ordered something different. Babe will be upset if she ever finds out.

"Of course I didn't. Babies become adult vermin. Plus they are just as dangerous as adults because they are born with that acid. Porky almost died from one of them. He was inspecting a site that had a normal cockroach infestation when one of the babies rolled out of a hidden nest, saw the Warty, and sprayed acid at his eyes. Luckily, the babies aim was slightly off from eight meters away and sprayed the side of his face and shoulder. If it had been a few centimeters closer to his eyes, his throat would have been hit and he would have bled out."

"Okay, well I will see you at home. Thanks for dinner," you say as you walk to your hovercraft.

"Don't forget to use your autopilot," Mom nags.

"I won't."

Not after this morning's accident.

10

As the hovercraft door closes, you hear them start fighting again. You turn on a video station while the autopilot starts driving home. A Warty in a business suit is sitting in front of you. He is hunched over with his hooves covering his eye.

"Are you tired of being unappreciated at work?" an announcer asks. "Do sows pass you by without even considering you? It is time to do something about your situation."

The Warty raises his head to the announcer's words. A smoke bomb goes off, masking the Warty. As the smoke clears, it is revealed that the Warty now has tusks twice the original size. He is also surrounded by two attractive sows, has a suit pocket full of credits, and a big smile on his face.

"Enlarz is an all natural herbal supplement that is clinically proven to lengthen your tusks. Stop being overlooked at work.

Stop being ignored by sows. Start taking Enlarz today."

Yeah, right. Let's see them grow a tusk on a Pigian, and then I will believe it.

Babe is calling you. You shut off the video station and answer, "Great timing. I was just thinking of you. How are you doing?"

"Could be better. How are you doing?" she asks.

"I can't complain too much."

"How was your dinner?"

"It wasn't that great. My parents fought for most of it."

"I am sorry to hear that," Babe says. "Do you remember my friend Pippo, the vegetarian?"

Oh shit.

"I ended up telling her about our lunch conversation, including what your dinner plans were tonight. She decided to go to The Slaughterhouse, too. I was upset when I found out what she did, but she told me something interesting."

I am so screwed. I knew that girl looked familiar.

"What did she say?"

"She ended up seeing you at the restaurant and she was shocked by what you ordered..."

"Yeah, I ended up getting my usual from there. I took our earlier conversation very seriously, but after this horrible day, I wanted something that I knew I would like."

"She said you had them take back your first order and got something completely different."

"Well, they ended up overcooking my charred toddler, so they offered me some Irish veal. I couldn't pass up the opportunity."

"You are telling me that you had an innocent toddler killed for no reason and you ate a fetus that was prematurely ripped out of its mother?"

"Not exactly, the toddler wasn't innocent. I picked the meanest one they had. He pushed a little girl off the seesaw."

"So that merited the kid being roasted alive? What did the fetus do? Kick its mother too much from the womb?"

"More than likely. You know how those fetuses get."

"Wilbur, this isn't funny."

"I know it isn't, but I don't know what to tell you."

"I love you, but I can't continue with this relationship if you continue to eat meat. I wish I could, but I can't. It is killing me inside. I keep thinking about the lives that were sacrificed as a part of your meal. I am not trying to pressure you into becoming vegetarian, that is a decision you have to make, but I am warning you that this relationship will not last if you stay on this path."

She is doing a very good job of pressuring me for not trying. Squealer called it. She gave the ultimatum the very same day he wondered about it.

"Are you telling me I have to choose right now?"

"No, you don't have to right now. There is no set timetable for this. The only thing I can say for certain is that I will not move off planet with you if you are still eating meat."

"Babe, I love you and don't want to lose you, but I don't know how to respond to your ultimatum."

"It isn't an ultimatum," she replies.

"Yes, it is. You are telling me either I give up meat or this relationship is going to end."

"No, I am telling you that your choice to eat meat is tearing me up inside and that I can't see our relationship working out if you continue to do so. It isn't an ultimatum, just a warning. I can't force you to become a vegetarian and expect our relationship to work. That isn't fair to you."

"Okay, well thanks for the warning; I guess. I will definitely think about it. I will talk to you later."

Please just end this conversation already. I have had enough drama for one day.

"Okay, good night, I love you" Babe says.

"I love you, too. Good night," you say

before disconnecting.

Is it too much to ask for one day without bickering parents and girlfriend drama? Just one peaceful day would be nice for a change.

You turn on a video station to try to relax. It is a commercial for eating man, which shows multiple delectable ways the meat can be cooked. It is one of your favorites which always ends with the catch phrase "Man: It's What's for Dinner."

God really has a cruel sense of humor sometimes.

The hovercraft pulls into your driveway. You turn off the video station and go inside. Spike is sleeping on his cushion in the utility room. The cushion isn't very big, but he manages to keep his arms and legs curled up on it. You gently scratch him behind the ear and then go into the kitchen. He is out of food and water, so you get him some more, just in case he wakes up before needing to be caged.

Did Dad say he was going to take care of the squatters? I wonder what he meant by that.

Mom enters the kitchen. Her lips are pursed and her eyes are squinting. Probably not the best time to talk to her, but you don't have much of a choice.

"Any idea where Dad is?"

"He is in the back shed," she snarls while exiting the kitchen.

Somebody was fighting the whole drive back.

You walk to the shed where your Dad has retrieved his pulse rifle and ground blind.

"So when you said you are going to deal with the squatters, you meant you're going to shoot them?"

"Yes, if those humans come by tonight, I am going to blow their brains out," Dad says.

That is better than any couples therapy you can get, but still...

"Do you have to kill them? Can't you trap them and then release them into one of the barriers?"

"What has gotten into you today? First you try to defend some baby shrews and now some human vermin. No, I am not going to capture them alive. I am going to kill them and then use their meat for tomorrow's dinner. Stop being a little sow."

"Why do you need to kill them? The only thing they do is sleep in our backyard at night."

"I am exterminator. How does it look if I have a squatter infestation? If we allow them to camp here at night, they will come back with friends and setup permanent residence here. I can't have that, so either grow a pair and help me or go back inside and bake me some cupcakes."

Moving off the planet just keeps looking better and better.

You walk back inside and go to your

room. You start working on your medical terminology assignment that is due tomorrow. Trying to focus is not easy after recent events. Every time you are close to an answer, Babe's conversation pops back into your head or the events of today's reeling trip, and you have to start all over again. The thirty minute assignment turns into a two hour ordeal, but eventually persistence does pay off.

Now that I am done with that torture, do I start on the essay for my Modern History class? Yeah, right, who am I kidding? That isn't due till Thursday, which means I won't start on it till Wednesday.

Instead of focusing on homework or your relationship issues, you start playing the game Darkgrog the Incinerator 6. In it, you are a dragon whose sole purpose in life is to pillage towns and kidnapping virgins. As you destroy castles and consume peasants, you level up based on the amount of gold you consume, which grants you points to unlock powers or upgrade existing ones. Babe would not approve of its lack of respect for life, but it is an effective way to relieve stress. Your favorite part about it is through the nanosuit you can see out of the eyes of the dragon, so when you shoot a fireball or chomp off the head of a peasant it feels real.

It is already 2 am? Where did the time go?

You walk over to the nanosuit station, deposit the nanomites for recharging, and then crawl into bed. Sleep does not come easy despite the late hour. Every thought that you tried to repress comes back as a ghost to haunt your waking hours just before slumber.

Eventually, you fall asleep.

You are being chased again, but this time the feral humans are riding Darkgrog, the behemoth black dragon from your video game. They also managed to fuse Jolters onto the beast's back, which means both giant fireballs and electrified harpoons are being shot at you. You run through the streets of Chicago trying to avoid your certain death. The dragon crashes into the different skyscrapers sending rubble down to crush you, but you manage to escape the debris. The fallen garage is up ahead. If you can get under there, you know everything will be okay. The dragon sees your plan and starts shooting the fireballs in front of your path. One of the blasts catches your arm on fire, but you use your nanosuit to extinguish it. You run around a vehicle as one of the feral humans accidently hits it with a harpoon. The electricity ignites the vehicle's fuel cell causing it to explode. The blast launches you through a window. When you stand back up, you discover you are back in your bedroom. All the distractions of Chicago, the feral humans, and the dragon have vanished.

There are two doors in front of you. The door to the right leads outside to the beach where Babe is waiting for you as the sun starts to set. She looks beautiful in her black bikini, but she also looks like she is getting tired of waiting on you. The door to the left leads to a dinner table where a roasted human rests on a dinner plate. The human has an apple in his mouth, cucumber slices over his eyes, and an onion blossom on top of his head. The smell of the roast makes your mouth salivate. The question is which door do you take?